Harry Clary Jones

Determination of the Atomic Weight of Cadmium

and the preparation of certain of its subcompounds

Harry Clary Jones

Determination of the Atomic Weight of Cadmium
and the preparation of certain of its subcompounds

ISBN/EAN: 9783337339791

Printed in Europe, USA, Canada, Australia, Japan

Cover: Foto ©Andreas Hilbeck / pixelio.de

More available books at **www.hansebooks.com**

Determination of the Atomic Weight
of Cadmium and the Preparation of
Certain of its Salt-Compounds.

Dissertation,

Presented to the Board of University Studies
of the
Johns Hopkins University,

for the Degree of

Doctor of Philosophy

By

Harry C. Jones

Contents.

Acknowledgment.

It affords me great pleasure to extend my sincere thanks to Professor Somerville for his instruction and personal interest during my entire connection with the University; to Dr. Ward, under whose immediate guidance the work described in this dissertation was completed; to Dr. Ernest for valuable assistance in qualitative chemistry and to Dr. Williams, with whom the branches of mineralogy and geology were followed as coordinate subjects.

Determination of the Atomic Weight
of
Cadmium.

Introduction and Historical Statement.

A careful examination of the literature on the atomic weight of cadmium will convince any one that considerable uncertainty yet remains in reference to this constant. Six experimenters have worked on this problem but the results of no one of them can be accepted as being more accurate than those of all others. The value assigned to cadmium varies from 111.48 to 112.32 on the basis of oxygen = 16. The best work has apparently been done by von Hauer, Lenssen and Huntington. The results of these three seem entitled to about equal confidence, yet the figure obtained by von Hauer differs from that of Huntington by three tenths of a unit.

The more prominent difficulties which
have been encountered were:

First. The preparation of aluminum compounds
free from all impurities, and which at the
same time were well adapted to weighing.

Second. The lack of a thoroughly simple
and exact method for the analysis of
aluminum compounds.

Third. Insufficient care in weighing in
many cases whereby small errors were
introduced into the results.

The methods which have been employed
are:

   Conversion of the metal into the oxide.
   (Thomsen.)

2 Conversion of the sulphate into the sulphide.
   (... and Partridge).

3 Decomposition of the ... to the oxide.
   (... and Partridge).

4 Determination of the chlorine in cadmium
chloride, by which the relation between the
chloride and metallic silver was established.
    (Lumox.)
5 Precipitation of the bromine in cadmium
bromide as silver bromide. (Huntington.)
6 The conversion of the oxalate into the oxi-
    ,oxide. (Partridge.)

The different pieces of work will be taken up
in chronological order and briefly considered.

Stromeyer, Schweigg. Journ 22. 366. 818.
determined the atomic weight of cadmium
a short time after the discovery of the element. He does not describe his method in
detail but established the relation between
cadmium and oxygen & is;
            Cd. O = 1.0. 14.352.

of the atomic weight : oxygen = .61

" : cadmium = 1.—83.

The very low result as compared with all subsequent work was probably due to the presence of a small amount of zinc, since the cadmium used was obtained from zinc ore and no adequate means of separation from the zinc is described.

von Hauer, Journ. f. prakt. Chem. 72, 338. 1857. His method consisted in reducing a weighed amount of cadmium sulphate to the sulphide in a stream of hydrogen sulphide, under pressure, at an elevated temperature, and weighing the sulphide. The reduction was shown to be complete by proving the absence of sulphate in the sulphide.

64. 2·051 grams of cadmium sulphate gave ⋅4.4471 sulphide.

... The atomic weight of copper = 0.

sulphur = 32.059.

cadmium = 111.?35.

The atomic weight of cadmium calculated in the manner of the more determinations made using the above values for copper and sulphur = ...?+

Maximum. .2.2.

Minimum. . .796.

Mean. ?+0.

The work of our James is greater to be without to that of Stromeyer. The large amount of material used in each de-termination tended to lessen any experi-mental error. A very considerable degree of care seems to have been exercised in pu-rifying the cadmium sulphate. In determinations - of a different specimen of sulphate was employed from that

...in determinations 6–9. The average time found in the first five determinations ... 910, in the last four = ... 977. The ... agreement between the results obtained from the different preparations ... The ... ...ate ... in favor ... a ... degree ... ... the material.

The method of weighing the more or less ... cadmium sulphate ... ... when employed in accurate work. The cadmium sulphate was placed in a ... and dried until ... ... and weighed. It was again ... ... as before, and weighed. The ... weighing ... be quickly ... ... the approximate weight was known. ... the weighings agreed to within one ... ... a milligram ... a third ... and weighing were made. In ...

a milligram in the weight of the cri-
terate gained an average error in the
atomic weight of cadmium of about .06.
That a discrepancy of greater or less magni-
tude was introduced from one source
will be readily seen.

Dinge   Ann. Chem. Pharm. 3, 55, 58. 1859.
determined the relation between cadmium
chloride and the metallic silver required to
precipitate the chlorine. Metallic cadmium
was dissolved in boiling hydrochloric
acid and the solution evaporated. The
cadmium chloride was fused for one
or two hours in a stream of hydrochloric
acid gas. Six determinations were made.
23.0645 grams of cadmium chloride were
equivalent to 27.73 grams metallic
silver.

Of the atomic weight of silver = .107.93.

                  chlorine = 35.45

                  cadmium = , 2.322.

The atomic weight of cadmium calculated as the average of the six determinations made, using the above values for
silver and chlorine = .12.241.

           Maximum, .2.757.

           Minimum, ..756.

           Mean,   2.241.

The wide difference between the results
would indicate some undesirable source
of error in part or all of the determinations. The first three determinations
were made from a different specimen
of cadmium from the last three.
In the first three the cadmium used
were first seen to have been purified and
the cadmium chloride prepared from it

...more or less tinted brown. In the last three a new specimen of metal was used which in a manner impossible could ... be compared to in examining ... The chloride prepared from it was ... well crystallized and ... ... water. In order to show clearly the wide discrepancy between the results obtained from the two specimens of cadmium which were used, the separate determinations are given in detail.

	CdCl$_2$	Ag.	at. wt. cadmium
1	2.369	2.791	112.322
2	4.540	5.348	112.347
3	6.177	7.260	112.759
4	2.404	2.941	111.756
5	3.5325	4.166	112.135
6	4.042	4.767	112.30

The average of the last three determinations = 2.450

The average of the last three determinations = 2.007.

From Dumas' own statement concerning the purity of the cadmium chloride analyzed, determinations 4–6 are ~~greater~~ to be preferred to determinations 1–3 and the most probable value from Dumas work would be very nearly 112.

Lenssen (pogg. ann. + Ann. Chem. 79, 281. 1860) regarded the oxalate of cadmium as well adapted to the determination of the atomic weight of cadmium. A solution of cadmium chloride which had been purified by repeated crystallisation was treated with an excess of a solution of pure oxalic acid. The cadmium oxalate formed was filtered off, washed, and carefully dried in the air at 150° C. until the last trace of water was removed.

.5697 grams cadmium oxalate gave .0047 grams cadmium oxide.

If the atomic weight of oxygen = 16.

carbon = 12.703.

cadmium = 12.043.

The average of the three determinations using the above values for oxygen and carbon is 12.067

Maximum, 12.304

Minimum, 11.911

Mean, 12.067.

The small amount of material used in each determination, the small number of determinations made, and the rather large difference between the highest and lowest result are objectionable. There are certain weak points in the method but to these reference will be made later.

Huntington, Proc. Amer. Acad. 17, 28. 1882.

working with Cooke, made two series of determinations of the atomic weight of cadmium. In the first series the relation between cadmium bromide and the silver bromide formed from it was determined. In the second, the relation between cadmium bromide and the silver required to precipitate the bromine.

The cadmium bromide was prepared in dissolving the carbonate in hydrobromic acid and subliming the product in a stream of carbon disulfide.

In the first series of eight determinations 23.3275 grams of cadmium bromide were equivalent to 32.2098 grams of silver bromide. So the atomic weight of silver = 107.93.

bromine = 79.95.

cadmium = 112.239

Maximum, 2.290.

Minimum, 2.69.

Where the difference between the maximum and minimum is slight the average of the separate determinations agrees closely with the number found by comparing the total substance used with the total product obtained. The latter method of calculation seems however to be preferable.

In the second series of eight determinations 28.6668 grams of cadmium bromide were equivalent to 22.7379 grams of silver.

Using the same values for silver and bromine the atomic weight of cadmium = 112.240.

Maximum, 2.320.

Minimum, 12.180.

The agreement of the separate determinations with each other is fairly close and the average of the two series of determinations is

... the same institution and great
... in the examination of his material
and in the carrying out of his method,
which are strong arguments in favor of
his work, yet his method is not so simple as could be desired where the nature
of the work demands the greatest possible
accuracy in all details and it also ex-
poses the subject to some of the errors com-
mon to ordinary analytical operations.

Partridge. Amer. Journ. Science XL, 377. 1890.
Methods: 1st. Decomposition of the oxalate to the
oxide. 2nd Reduction of the sulphate to the
sulphide. 3rd Conversion of the oxalate into the
sulphide. The average of ten determinations
made by each method gives (Partridge)
1st series. atomic weight of cadmium ... 111.807.
2nd   "   :   ... 111.790?.

3rd series. Atomic weight of cadmium = .[?]000.

An excellent agreement between results obtained by different methods?

That this very close agreement is only apparent has been shown by [?]. It was found that these [?] calculations are based on the assumption that the atomic weight of carbon = 12, and that of sulphur = 32 when oxygen = 16. There seems to be little justification for this rather arbitrary selection by [Partridge] since the most refined work shows that whole numbers do not express the most probable atomic weights of carbon and sulphur in a system where oxygen = 16.

The atomic weight of cadmium calculated from the total material used and the total product found in each of the three series is:

Mean from [?] 3. 3[?]. 8[?].

$$O = 16. \quad C = 12. \quad S = 32. \quad \text{at. wt. ed.}$$

Cd_2O_4	$CdO =$	$2.603632 : 8.10031\tfrac{1}{2}$	$111.800.$
$CdSO_4$	$CdS =$	$6.935632 : 1.020212$	$111.780.$
CdC_2O_4	$CdO =$	$6.850232 : 2.12906\tfrac{1}{2}$	$111.800.$

$$\text{difference,} \quad .020.$$

$$O = 16. \quad C = 12.003. \quad S = 32.059 \quad \text{at. wt. ed.}$$

Cd_2O_4	$CdO =$	$2.603632 : 8.100312.$	$111.8.0.$
$CdSO_4$	$CdS =$	$6.935632 : 1.020212.$	$.787.$
CdC_2O_4	$CdS =$	$6.850232 : 2.29762.$	$111.610.$

$$\text{difference,} \quad 0.200.$$

As Harte has pointed out when these values
are drawn for carbon and sulphur which
are founded on the best experimental evidence the agreement between the different
series of results as calculated by Partridge is
somewhat modified.

I have repeated the work on which series 1

... with and would ... attention to
the ... in much to ...
... to have been experimental[ly]
distin...

1. The metal was ... distilled three in a
vacuum. It has been found in this ...
... that ... ... cadmium or
zinc can be prepared ... by repeated distillations, each one ... to ...
... the impurities to ... by
means of their difference in volatility.

2. The ... mixture of metal and
oxide resulting from the decomposition of the
... was then moistened with a few
... of nitric acid in order to oxidize
any reduced metal. Unless the ...
... of metal and oxide was dissolved
there would be danger of the presence of
free undissolved metal which would

...the temperature of decomposition of cadmium nitrate. An appreciable loss in weight resulting from a distillation of the metal out of the crucible might arise result.

6 It seems very probable that the cadmium nitrate was not heated sufficiently to remove all traces of the oxides of nitrogen. I have found that this could only be accomplished by long continued heating. Constant weight was not sufficient to have decided this point since it was also found that this could be reached short of complete decomposition, or the temperature was too low to remove the last traces of the oxides. Some very delicate test for such oxides should have been applied at the end of each experiment.

The following table contains a summary of the results thus far obtained.

Where two values are given for one series of determinations, the first is calculated from the total material used and the total period round, the second is an average of the results of the separate experiments. Oxygen is taken as a standard.

Date.	Authority.	At. wt. Cd.
8 …	Stromeyer.	..—83
857.	von Hauer.	…935 ⎱
		…9—0 ⎰
859.	Dumas.	112.322 ⎱
		112.2—. ⎰
860.	Lenssen.	12.0—3 ⎱
		112.0—7 ⎰
882.	Huntington, 1st series	12.23?
	" ", 2nd	.2.145

Investigation

Partridge, ... 05

2nd .. 780

3rd . 0

... Partridge's results

... = 32. ...

... 32.059

Partridge, ... 6

2nd .. 27

3rd .. 6.0.

After a careful examination of the methods ... it became evident that no one of them was far as accurate as the method employed by ... and Burton, in the determination of the atomic weight of ..., and more recently by Burton and ..., in the determination of the atomic weight of magnesium. The

method ... ... the pure some ... cadmium, to ... a weighed ... ... the ... ... by means ... ... and, to ... the ... ... to ... and to weigh the ...

Preparation of Pure Cadmium.

The work of preparing pure cadmium was begun more than two years ago by Mr. W. V. Metcalf with Dr. H. N. Morse. I wish to express here my sincere thanks to him for the material with which the following determinations were made. The cadmium used by him was obtained from Schuchart and marked "Met. ... ..." The method of purification by fractional distillation in a vacuum, was essentially

that was employed by Marie and Bunsen for the ... of ... ...

The distillation was carried out in hard glass tubes ... the aid of ... ...

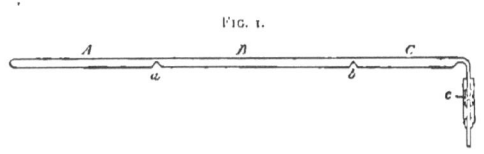

FIG. 1.

Fig. 1. represents such a tube. A hard glass tube, ... in length, was ... at one end and about 30 grams of cadmium introduced. The walls of the tube were heated and indented at two points a, and b, with a red-hot ..., dividing the tube into three sections marked A, B and C. The open end of the tube was drawn out, bent, and attached to a Sprengel air-pump by means of a rubber tube.

The joint was tied tightly with waxed cord and surrounded by mercury. When the manometer indicated that the tube was exhausted, it was gradually heated by the combustion furnace in which it rested. The metal in A melted and distilled slowly into the front portion of the tube. Most of it condensed in B, while a small part, together with any more volatile impurities, collected in C which was kept cooler than the remainder of the tube. When about four-fifths of the metal placed in A had distilled over, the tube was very slowly cooled. When cold, the tube was broken open, the portions in A and C being rejected in every case, while the metal was removed from B in the form of a bar resting on the bottom of the tube, together with some crystal aggregates.

suspended from the top and sides. A few crystal ... were ... but the measurement of these will be considered later. The metal deposited from the ... with a ... lustrous surface and had not attacked the glass in the least.

The next distillation was ... in a tube ... as represented in fig 1, but drawn out at each end. The original cadmium powder was heated in the tube in a stream of ... hydrogen gas, for the purpose of 'skimming' the metal in the form of bars, and to reduce any cadmium oxide contained in the powder.

Six distillations were made in a vacuum. In the first, 630 grams of metal were used being distilled in quantities of about 30 grams each. At the end of the sixth distillation, there were about 75

grams of pure cadmium at disposal.
In the fifth and sixth distillations, the
metal was heated just above the melting
point by twenty to twenty-one hours,
were being forced over into the residue
portion of the tube. By this means
all the remaining traces of the more
volatile atoms were driven into the front
part of the tube and separated from
the cadmium.

The distillations.
The residue represents the undistilled portion remaining in A. The distillate, the
material obtained from B after the distillation was exhibited. The coating, the
substance which condensed in C.

Residue. Cd, Pb, Zn, Ag.
Distillation = distillate. Cd, Zn, Ag.
Coating. Cd, Zn, Ag.

The distillate from the last distillation ... was ... and spectroscopium ... ... examined and found to be free ... ... The .... was more minute than the spectroscope and thus failed to reveal a trace.

The Preparation of Pure Nitric Acid.

The method of preparing the pure acid and of measuring and transferring it was the same as adopted by Morse and Burton in their work on the atomic weight of ...

FIG. 2.

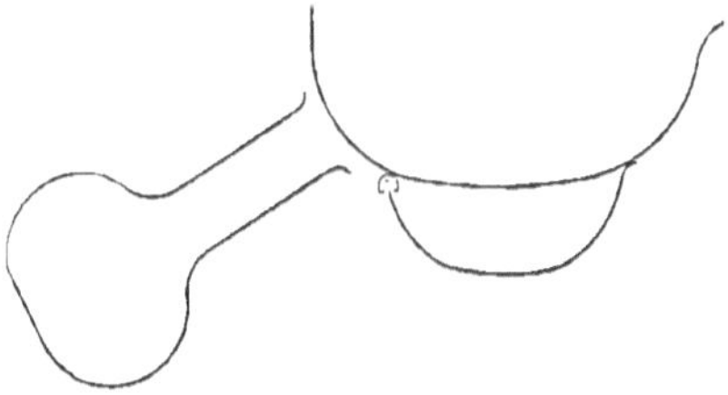

The ... form ... apparatus is represented in fig. 2 ... A ... retort will containing fragments of ... was connected to a smaller retort tube, into which
it was separated by ... the large retort-
... was ... The acid was distilled from
a small flask as represented in the
drawing.

The purest nitric acid which could be
obtained was diluted with about an
equal volume of water. The ... containing the acid was heated very gently
that the distillation might take place
without ... The nitric acid condensed on the cold surface of the larger
... and collected in the smaller, in
which it was preserved until used.
This was ... to residue on evaporation.

The arrangement of crucibles.

Fig. 3.

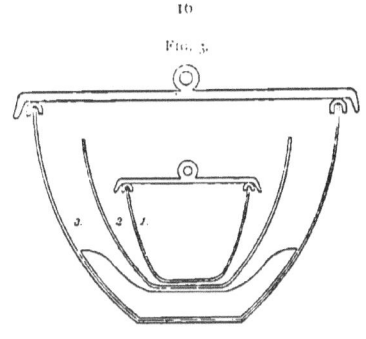

The arrangement of the ~~crucible~~ crucibles
in which the determinations were made is
represented in fig 3. It is a small platinum
crucible, (0) with the external and lid of
which the glaze had been removed by
platinous acid. The lid was separated from
the crucible by hooks made from thick
platinum wire, to allow free communication
between the contents of the crucible and the
external air. This would facilitate the
outward diffusion of the oxides of nitrogen

...was decanted from the nitrate. ... an
unweighed porcelain crucible (No. I) on
which ... rested. From the ... the
... had been ... to prevent the crucible from adhering to the unglazed porcelain crucible on which it rested. The
exterior was ... brushed ... treatment with hydrofluoric acid to remove
all ... particles adhering to its surface.
Crucibles 1 and 2 were not separated during
a determination.

3 is a nickel crucible about two and a half
inches in diameter. The porcelain crucibles
were not allowed to touch the nickel
at any point. The nickel crucible was
covered by a lid of nickel.

The mod..? ... Oxidation.

A piece of oxidation readings were two to three grains was cut from the bar of the metal by means of a steel chisel. This was ... with steel ... and filed with a hard steel file to about one half the original weight. Care was taken to remove the entire exterior portion of the metal which had come into contact with the chisel or had stood exposed to the air. The piece of metal was then carefully brushed and examined with a lens to ensure the removal of all loose particles from its surface.

Crucibles and a having been brought to constant weight against their tare, were ready for use. The piece of aluminium was weighed and placed in ... the excess of ... nitric acid was added and a gentle heat applied

until all the water was removed. This required from twenty to forty hours. A sand-bath was constructed by placing a large porcelain crucible on the iron crucible and filling the intervening space with sand. The pair of crucibles (fig 2) was placed in the porcelain crucible and the contents evaporated to dryness by warming very carefully at first and gradually increasing the temperature. The pair of crucibles was then transferred to a bath constructed as the above where iron-turnings took the place of sand. This ~~bath~~ was heated by a small burner until the nitrate was nearly decomposed. Then a triple burner was added and finally two for six or eight hours. This was found sufficient to effect complete decomposition. When cold the pair of crucibles was placed

.... the .... with great energy
and moved the crucible.

The decomposition of the nitrate was shown
to be complete not by constant weight alone,
but by testing for oxides of nitrogen with
starch paste rendered extremely sensitive
with potassium iodide. That the test should
be reliable, Morse and Burton have pointed
out that all the reagents used must be
free from oxidizing agents. The presence
of iodate in the iodide is especially to be
avoided. This was removed by boiling
the solution with zinc amalgam.
Air was removed from all the solutions
by boiling.

When the starch-potassium-iodide solution
had been prepared as sensitive as possible,
a portion of it was treated with a little
hydrochloric acid, to determine if any

iodine was liberated. If no coloration
was produced the cadmium oxide was added
it dissolved in the hydrochloric acid and
if any oxides of nitrogen were present they
would have revealed themselves by the
liberation of iodine and a blue coloration
of the starch paste.

In no one of the ten determinations was
the slightest coloration detected.

An equal volume of nitric acid was added
to the pair of crucibles used as a tare as to
those containing the determination, and they
were treated in exactly the same manner
and for the same length of time.

The crucibles containing the cadmium oxide
were heated over the blast-lamp an hour,
weighed against their tare, reheated.

... again weighed, and this continued until there was no further change in weight. Usually from two to four hours heating with the blast-lamp was sufficient to completely decompose the nitrate. The test for residual nitrogen was then applied.

... that practically constant weight could be reached short of complete decomposition, at a temperature below that necessary to transform all the nitrate into the oxide. This necessitated the final test for residual nitrogen.

The Weighing.

The balance used was a No. 8 long-armed one, made by Becker and Sons. It was supported by iron brackets fastened to one of the foundation walls of the laboratory.

here it would be connected to the mast jar
and was also well protected from air
currents. All weighings were made between the hours of one and six in the
morning when the surroundings were
as quiet as could be desired. A very slight
disturbance was detected by the vibrations
of the surface of a cup of mercury
placed experimentally between the parts

That the presence of the operator
might not produce any change in the
balance during the weighing, he used
the arm, placed the weight above and removed his head and took his position in
front of the balance at least an hour
before making a weighing. When his
presence no longer affected the balance (which
was shown by the zero point remaining
practically constant in a series of determinations)

The weighing was rapid. The method of weighing by substitution and using both bars was employed throughout.

Each zero point was taken as the mean of three six in agreeing zero determinations; each one of the three being the mean of seven readings. The zero of the balance empty was determined just before and after each weighing to detect any change in its position. Generally none was observed. The sensibility of the balance was taken at each weighing with the weights used at that weighing. A displacement of the zero point about six divisions of the mm scale was effected by the addition of one milligram.

The weights had been specially adjusted and were carefully compared with each other before using.

...weighing of them was adopted in preference to any other method. By this means all errors resulting from changes in the moisture of the air were avoided and any errors which might have been introduced by heating or manipulating the crucible would be counteracted by treating the tare in exactly the same manner.

Taring the Crucibles.

A pair of crucibles (and 2 in the figure) was selected and treated as described. Another pair about the same size but a little lighter was prepared in exactly the same way. Each tare was placed in the nickel crucible and heated by means of the blast-lamp for half an hour.

After drying in desiccators with care the
crucibles were placed in the closed balance
until no longer affected by the moisture
of the air, which was also dried by cal-
cium chloride. The tare was brought to
within one tenth of a milligram of the
weight of the crucibles against which it
was being tared, by adding fragments of
porcelain obtained from another crucible
of the same composition. The difference
in weight between the tare and its mate
was then accurately ascertained.
Each pair of crucibles was again placed
in the nickel crucible and blasted for
half an hour. They were then reweighed,
to determine if the difference in weight
previously found had remained constant.
In no case was any change detected,
yet this precaution was always taken.

The Results.

The following table contains the results of the foregoing determinations.

		at int ed.	at int ed.
	wt. of CaO.	$(O = 16)$	$(O = 15.96)$
1.77891	2.03288	112.070	111.790
.92492	2.18544	112.078	111.778
.74685	1.99620	112.078	111.778
.50700	1.797.8	112.053	777.3
.48748	2.20820	2.061	111.781
2.54247	2.59731	112.089	111.779
.55825	2.00775	112.180	111.816
.73128	1.94305	112.057	111.779
.92237	2.19677	112.183	111.803
.92081	2.19502	2.078	111.778

Means ..2.0705. ...77.05.

Maximum,	2.18.	..880.
Minimum,	2.053.	.773
Difference,	.133	..133.

Calculating the atomic weight of cadmium from the total amount of metal used and base found, we have:

$$\text{At. Wt. of Cd.} \qquad \text{At. Wt. of Cd}$$
$$(O = 16) \qquad (O = 16.96)$$
$$.2570. \qquad 11.7704.$$

These results agree more closely with those of von Hauer and Lenssen than with those of any other experimenter. The following table gives a comparison of the work of this investigation with that herein described:

[illegible]	[illegible]	[illegible]
[illegible] determinations.	3 determinations.	10 determinations
(O = 16	(O = 16)	(O = 16)
[illegible]	2.067	2.07[illegible]
2.[illegible]	2.304	2.080
[illegible]	[illegible]	2.003
.326	.393	.033.

A difference of three or four tenths of a unit between the different results of a [illegible] leaves considerable doubt as to the accuracy of the method employed and to the value obtained.

The figure elected by [illegible], as most probable for the atomic weight of cadmium is [illegible]2.[illegible]8. This is the mean of the results of von Hauer and [illegible]. They were much [illegible] to

Objections to the method.

It was shown that zinc oxide can be heated in a platinum vessel in a muffle furnace, to the melting point of steel, without undergoing any dissociation, or in any way losing in weight. This source of error was avoided by using porcelain vessels, which were not in contact with the free flame.

The statement of Marignac that the oxide of zinc derived from the nitrate retains oxides of nitrogen even when heated to the temperature at which it begins to undergo dissociation, was shown by the same authors to be without foundation. The basis of this objection is doubtless to be found in the imperfect method of testing for such oxides.

It might be urged as an objection to this method that the difference in weight between the metal and oxide is not very great, therefore any error in weighing would be multiplied in the result. At first sight this objection may appear valid, but since the substances weighed were so well adapted to that purpose and the weighings could be made with such a high degree of accuracy no appreciable error could have resulted from this source.

A crucible with its contents was repeatedly weighed against its tare and weights to ascertain the difference between successive weighings under the conditions employed. A number of weighings agreed to .0002 gr. and in some instances to half this amount.

Advantages of the Method.

1. The great advantage of the method is its extreme simplicity. From the beginning of an experiment until the end the contents of the crucible are not brought into contact with any foreign substance. By this means small errors resulting from incomplete precipitation, or filtration and all other errors incident to ordinary processes of analysis were avoided.

2. The nature of the metal and its oxide rendered them well adapted to weighing. The specific gravity of the metal and oxide approached so closely to that of the weights, that it was unnecessary

The Nitrate Method.

The method consists in taking a
weighed amount of [...] nitrate
decomposing it by heat, when a mixture
of [...] and nitrite are said to be formed
[...] this mixture in nitric acid,
[...] the nitrate into [...] and
weighing the oxide.

[...] obtained results by this
method which agree very closely with
those recorded in the earlier part of
this dissertation.
Working with the same method,
[...] arrived at a value
[...] of a unit [...]
than that of [...].

It appeared advisable that the method should be revisited with the greatest care to ascertain what result it would give under the most favorable conditions.

Having a quantity of acid [admixture] it was necessary to prepare pure oxalic acid.

Preparation of Pure Oxalic Acid.

The commercial acid was crystallised three times from cold water to separate it from acid [sulphate]. It was then boiled for two days with a 15 per cent solution of hydrochloric acid, to remove any mineral matter present. The acid which crystallised from the hydrochloric acid solution was recrystallised ~~from~~ twice from distilled water, and then

... . It was finally heated
with water to remove any ... ...
and ... crystallized ... water.
The ... dried in the air at ordinary
temperatures. ... ... no residue on
ignition.

Preparation of Cadmium Oxalate.

A ... of cadmium was dissolved in ...
nitric acid. On evaporating the
solution, cadmium nitrate was obtained.
Twenty-one grams of the nitrate were
dissolved in 750 c.c. of redistilled water.
Somewhat less than an equivalent of the
oxalic acid was dissolved in an equal
volume of water, and slowly added to the
solution of the nitrate with constant
shaking. A little less than an equivalent of oxalic acid was used to avoid

...tending to ... acid ...
... acid was precipitated on
standing a few minutes as a white
crystalline compound, ... subjected to
washing. The ... was ... and
washed until the wash water was free
from all traces of nitric acid. It was
then washed ... times with water which
had been twice redistilled and ... in
... for twenty hours at 50°C.

The arrangement of the crucibles which
were weighed was in all respects like
that in the preceding method.

Mode of Procedure.

The crucibles were heated, dried and
weighed exactly as in the preceding method

The ... was ... on ground-
... supports three ... which ...
... connected to the ... of the two
... crucibles. The ... of crucibles
(1 and 2 ... 3) was placed in a third por-
... crucible and the whole system im-
... into an upright air-bath. The
... crucible was supported on a porcelain triangle about an inch from the
bottom of the bath and was not allowed
to touch the ... at any point. The
top of the bath was covered with a sheet
of ... ... which was ... an asbestos board. The external was also ...
with a ... of asbestos. A thermom-
eter was introduced well into the bath.
The temperature was allowed to rise slowly
until the ... began to show a ...
... ... the edge. From this stage

The temperature was kept as low as possible in order to effect the concentration. When the result was concentrated the water was allowed to boil and the solution of the crucible completely dissolved in nitric acid. The nitrate was evaporated to dryness and determined as in the method but described. The end of the concentration was determined in the same manner and the oxide, after being all dissolved, weighed.

The drying and weighing of the oxide.

It was necessary to dry the oxide before weighing took within 2 twenty hours at 50° C. the addition to the twenty hours depends of the whole operation. At low temperature the last trace of moisture

...were removed by .... heating.

The melting of the zeolite was made in the melting .... in ...... it was fixed. The two .... had been .... against each other, ... the weights of the ..... and ...... between fragments of glass to it until the difference in weight was a small fraction of a milligram. The zeolite having been ...... to constant weight, was weighed. It was then ...... in ......, and .... from the melting ...... with the crucible and the glass again weighed against its tare. The difference in the two weights gave the amount of zeolite. The glass and its tare were ...... and re-weighed to determine if the two milligrams of zeolite adhering to the ......

The Results

The method be carried out whereas the
extract ... any changes occurred with
the salt ... it was weighed.

Disadvantages of the Method.

1 The rapidity with which the said extract
takes up moisture from the air is an
objection to its use in the determination of
atomic weights. Even with the greatest care
there is a certain element of uncertainty
introduced from this source.

2 The extract is stated to decompose into a
mixture of the oxide and nitric. The
temperature required for this decomposition
is considerably higher than the melting
point of cadmium. The metals heated in
the melting point possess a vapour-pressure

and less in every must result,
whatever precaution is taken in
heating. This is the probable explana-
tion why the results obtained by
this method are lower than those of
the preceding.

A comparison of the two methods leads
me to attach much more impor-
tance to the results of that one which
establishes the relation between cadmium and cadmium oxide directly
and I therefore regard the atomic
weight of cadmium as very closely
expressed by the figure 112·07 when
Oxygen = 16

Preparation of Certain Salt-compounds
of
Cadmium.

Historical

Cadmium acts so generally as a bivalent element that it is usually regarded as entering into combination only where it can have that role. The other compound described, in which it has apparently a lower valence than two, was prepared by Marchand[1]. It was obtained by heating cadmium oxalate to the mixture point of lead when a green powder remained behind which resembled chromium oxide. When heated in the air it appeared to be decomposed into metal and oxide. When treated with mercury the compound was not altered. The analysis showed it to have the composition represented by the formula Cd_2O.

R. Vogel[1] has shown that the green powder described by Marchand consists of a mixture of the metal and oxide. When this mixture is treated with dilute acetic acid the metal remains behind as microscopic glistening globules. The lower the temperature at which the oxalate is decomposed the more oxide and the less metal were found in the product.

There was then no compound known in which cadmium acted as if its valence was less than two when this work was undertaken.

That it may act with a greater valence was shown by R. Fraets[2]. He found that when zinc hydroxide was treated with hydrogen peroxide certain compounds of zinc and oxygen were formed containing

more oxygen than the normal oxide ZnO. The close relationship between zinc and cadmium lead him to try the same reaction with cadmium. Hydrogen peroxide was accordingly allowed to act on cadmium hydroxide and the resulting product analyzed. There were formed Cd_5O_6, Cd_3O_5 and Cd_4O_7. In no case was the compound CdO_2 obtained. These compounds are described as fairly stable even at a hundred degrees.

The Preparation of Cd_4Cl_7

When anhydrous cadmium chloride is heated with metallic cadmium in a vacuum, or in an atmosphere of nitrogen, to the fusing point of the chloride the molten

chloride quickly assumes a garnet red
colour. In order to investigate this phenomenon
a quantity of the chloride was prepared by
dissolving the redistilled metal in an excess of hydrochloric acid, evaporating the
chloride to dryness on a water bath, and
finally removing the water of crystallisation
by heating in a current of dry hydrochloric acid gas. The heating was effected
by placing the chloride in a long platinum boat, which was placed into a
large glass tube, through which was
passed a current of the acid gas. The
tube was heated by means of a combustion furnace and the chloride kept in
the molten condition for two or three
hours. By this means a perfectly
white crystalline chloride of the composition $CdCl_2$ was obtained, free from

water or oxychloride.

The chloride and an excess of metal were placed in a long-necked flask of hard glass and after the displacement of the air by nitrogen heated to the melting point of the chloride. The liquid chloride attained its maximum depth of color in a few minutes, nevertheless the heating was continued for one hours. When the temperature was allowed to rise much above the melting point of the chloride the red substance underwent decomposition and globules of metal collected upon the walls of the flask. For this reason no more heat was applied than was just necessary to keep the contents of the flask in a liquid condition. During the very gradual cooling of the flask it was shaken gently in order to

precipitate the existance of any metal
which might be mechanically retained
by the chloride.

In cooling the solidified mass possessed
a slightly greenish tint which disappeared when cold, the substance having
then a grayish white color and a
cleavage resembling that of talc or brucite.
When examined under the microscope
it was found to be perfectly homogeneous and free from metal. It gave no
metallic streak when rubbed between
agate surfaces.

The analysis of the first preparation
showed the following composition;

Amount of Chloride used ...... .3357 g.
" cadmium found ...... .2159 "
Chlorine " ...... .1198 "

Cadmium	Chlorine
64.27 per cent.	35.61 per cent.

These proportions are nearly those of a compound having the composition Cd_2Cl_3. in which the calculated percentages are:

Cadmium.	Chlorine.
64.34	35.66

(Foot note). In the paper in the American Chemical Journal XII. 488. which records this work the analyses and percentages were calculated on the basis of the atomic weight of cadmium = 111.7. Although my work since this date has shown that 112.07 is the true value, yet I think it preferable to use the old number here since the changes to be introduced would be very slight and the same results are thereby kept uniform in the two publications.

In order to determine whether the close
approximation to definite atomic proportions might not be accidental, the
material was ... with an excess of
the metal for twenty hours. The product
was analysed.

Amount of chloride used ....~59?0?
   Cadmium found .... .9390+..
   Chlorine " .... .52329..

 Cadmium.   Chlorine.
 64.33 per cent. 35.85 per cent.

A second preparation of the substance
was made in all respects like the first.
Two analyses were made.

First Analysis:

Amount of the Chloride used--- .????? ?
      Cadmium found.... .39235
      Chlorine   ----- .21725

Cadmium.   Chlorine.
64.31 per cent.   35.61 per cent.

Second Analysis:

Amount of the Chloride used--- .20616 9?
      Cadmium found..... .13260
      Chlorine " ..... .07352

Cadmium   Chlorine.
64.35 per cent.   35.66 per cent.

A third preparation was made like
the first and second and analyzed.

Analysis:

Amount of the chloride used ...... .2832 g.
            cadmium found ...... .18244 "
            chlorine "   ...... .10123 "

Cadmium.   Chlorine.
64.42 per cent.   35.74 per cent.

When the new substance is heated it
fuses to a red liquid and then breaks
up into metal and the chloride of cadmium. The reactions are in general
those of a strong reducing agent. Treated
with nitric acid, oxides of nitrogen are
liberated. With dilute hydrochloric,
sulphuric and acetic acids it gives

free hydrogen. In the presence of dilute hydrochloric acids it reduces mercuric to mercurous chloride, or to metallic mercury.

Three determinations of the reducing power of the substance were made with a freshly prepared specimen, by dissolving weighed portions in hydrochloric acid and measuring the hydrogen liberated.

The following results were obtained:

	hydrogen found.	hydrogen calculated for CdH_2
1st determination	15.67 c.c.	15.65 c.c.
2nd	11.80 c.c.	11.82 c.c.
3rd	23.10 c.c.	23.03 c.c.

An examination of the analyses shows beyond question that the substance formed by the action of metallic cadmium

... the molten anhydrous chloride in a ... definite composition. The ... of cadmium to chlorine would not be changed even when the substance was heated with the metal for twenty hours, while a very short time was sufficient for its formation when the metal and chloride were melted together.

It may be possible that a substance possessing these properties is not a definite chemical compound but a mixture of cadmium and cadmic chloride or a solution of one in the other.

If it were a solution it is difficult to see why the composition of the solution should be so constant, since the solubility of a substance is generally altered by a change in temperature. The different preparations were not made

at exactly the same temperature yet the composition of the different preparations was the same.

If the substance was a mixture of the two chlorides, when treated with water the cadmic chloride would most probably dissolve directly leaving the cadmous chloride to be acted upon by the water. The decomposition by water will however be seen not to be as simple as would be expected under these conditions.

From the above considerations it appears highly probable that the substance is a definite chemical compound of cadmic and cadmous chlorides. If cadmic chloride can form a chemical compound with the chloride of another element there appears to be no reason why it should not form a compound with

The preparation of $CdBr_2$.

The anhydrous bromide of cadmium was prepared by dissolving the carbonate in an aqueous solution of hydrobromic acid, evaporating the bromide to dryness on the water bath and heating the residue in a current of dry hydrobromic acid gas. When the bromide was heated with an excess of the metal in an atmosphere of nitrogen, it conducted itself, in general, like the chloride. When the molten bromide and the metal came into contact the salt quickly became deep red in color. After heating for some time considerable dissociation was produced by raising the temperature. This was more apparent in the preparation of the bromide than with the chloride. On

cooling. The mass possessed a greenish
tint which disappeared when cold. The
bromide thus being were nearly the same
color as the corresponding chloride. Like
the chloride it appeared to be homogeneous
and free from metal. Two determinations of
cadmium and two of bromine were made,
using the product as soon as prepared.

First determination of cadmium:
Amount of substance used.... .3730 gr.
        cadmium found...... .1658 ..
Cadmium.
    44.59 per cent.

Second determination of cadmium:
Amount of substance used .... .3593 gr.
        cadmium found......... .1603
Cadmium.
    44.57 per cent.

First determination of bromine:
Amount of substance used ...... .66640 gr.
" " bromine found ...... .36953 "
Bromine.
55.45 per cent.

Second determination of bromine:
Amount of substance used .... .56035 gr.
" " bromine found .... .31085 "
Bromine.
55.47 per cent.

The percentage of cadmium and bromine found agrees here closely with that of a compound of the formula $CdBr_2$. The relation of cadmium to bromine in this would be:

Cadmium.   Bromine.
44.44 per cent.   55.56 per cent

When this compound was heated for a long time with an excess of the metal its composition was not appreciably changed.

The compound Cd_4Br_7 is a strong reducing agent: giving with nitric acid oxides of nitrogen; with dilute hydrochloric, sulphuric or acetic acid, free hydrogen, and with mercuric chloride, mercurous chloride or metallic mercury. The action of water on the bromide by means of which cadmium hydroxide was formed, was not studied as carefully as with the chloride but appeared to be essentially the same.

The Preparation of $CdI_2 = 23$

Cadmic iodide was prepared in the same manner as the bromide. It was dried in a stream of hydriodic acid gas at as low temperature as possible to lessen the decomposition of the hydriodic acid. When the anhydrous iodide was heated with an excess of metal in an atmosphere of nitrogen the red color of the iodide became intensified. Heating was continued until there was evidence of dissociation, which, under the same conditions, was less marked than with the chloride and much less than with the bromide. Owing to the high specific gravity of the iodine compound some difficulty was experienced in obtaining a preparation free from metal. This difficulty was finally

overcome by keeping the material not above the solution temperature too a too time and crystallized during the heat. During the process of stirring a precipitate precipitate that was observed which disappeared as the process was continued. When cold the substance resembled the chloride and bromide. The determinations of cadmium were made on the first preparation.

First determination:
Amount of substance used ---- .55549 gr.
"   " cadmium found ..... .17456 " .
Cadmium.
31.43 per cent.

Second determination.
Amount of substance used --- .47636 gr
"   " cadmium found .... .14980 "

Cadmium. 31.5, per cent.

As these results did not correspond to the constitution represented by the formula CdI_2, which our experience with the chloride and bromide had led us to expect, we reheated the material in currents ... with an excess of the metal. Two analyses of the product gave:

Cadmium.	Iodine.
31.44 per cent.	68.65 per cent.
31.39 .	68.68 . .

Proving that the iodide had taken up during the first heating all the metal which it could retain. The analytical results suggest the formula $Cd_{12}I_{23}$, in which the calculated percentages are:

Cadmium   Iodine.

31.53   68.47

In its conduct towards dilute hydrochloric
and acetic acids and water, the substance
behaves like the corresponding chloride
and bromide.

The Preparation of Cadmous Hydroxide and Oxide.

When the substance Cd_2I_2 is treated with water a complicated reaction takes place. The general character of the reaction appears to be the same with the chloride, bromide and iodide. The decomposition of the chloride was studied more thoroughly than that of the other compounds.

When the easily powdered chloride is treated with water it yields cadmic chloride which passes into solution, a small quantity of a white insoluble material which may be cadmic hydroxide but which in no case could be entirely freed from traces of chlorine, and a highly lustrous crystalline substance which rapidly lost its crystalline appearance and passed over into a grayish white amorphous

compound, which when held from
chlorine was found to be cadmious hydroxide, of the formula Cd Cl. The separate
crystalline residues from the treatment
with water were analyzed

First analysis:

Amount of Cd Cl₂ treated with water 1.45970.9₂
Cadmium found in fluorescent precipitate 023.8
        crystalline substance ... .9614
        solution in water ... .81970
Total cadmium found - - - - - - - .93902

Chlorine found in crystalline compound .. .00371
       solution in water ...... .51671
Total chlorine found - - - - - - - .52042

Approximately seven-eighths of the total cadmium dissolved as cadmic iodide while the remainder was contained in the insoluble precipitate and in the gray crystalline compound.

Second analysis:

Amount of $CdCl_2$ treated with water... 1.0794 gr.
Cadmium found in insoluble precipitate... .01469
"   "   solution in water... .60795

Chlorine found in solution in water..... .35791

The percentage of cadmium in the white precipitate is less in this analysis than in the former. The cadmium in solution is again about seven-eighths of the total and the chlorine present in the same

solution shows that the cadmium was
all contained as cadmium chloride.

The attempts to determine the composition
of the gray crystalline compound failed,
owing to the rapidity with which it decomposed with water. Even with the
most rapid work it could not be
isolated in the undecomposed condition.
Moreover, the partially decomposed
crystals gave variable proportions of
water and halogen but never less than
eight equivalents of the former to one of
the latter.

While the decomposition of CdX with
water cannot at present be fully explained,
yet it is clear from the analyses that
the whole of the total cadmium is thrown
down as a white precipitate and a

crystalline compound which as will
be seen passes over into cadmium hydroxide. One half of the cadmium chloride
is oxidized to cadmic chloride using the
chlorine from the other half.

The compound Cd Cl was treated
directly with absolute alcohol with the
hope of obtaining the crystalline substance in an undecomposed condition.
Although a substance of the same general
appearance as that formed in the
presence of water was obtained yet it
decomposed so readily that a satisfactory analysis could not be made.

Notwithstanding the rapidity with which
the decomposition of the crystalline compound begins, long continued washing

was necessary in order to completely remove the chlorine. The extraction of the
last traces of the halogen is hastened by
the use of warm instead of cold water.
The temperature of the water must not
exceed 50°C. In water whose temperature
approaches the boiling point the hydroxide
is slowly decomposed with liberation
of water.

The new hydroxide is a strong reducing
agent. It dissolves in dilute acids;
yielding with nitric acid oxides of nitrogen
with hydrochloric or sulphuric acid
free hydrogen. After washing with warm
water until all the chlorine had disappeared, it was dried over phosphorus
pentoxide and analyzed.

First determination of cadmium.

Amount of substance used ------- .09892.

    cadmium found -------- .08415

    Cadmium

       86.93 per cent.

Second determination of cadmium.

Amount of substance used ---- .09856 gr.

    cadmium found ---- .08522

    Cadmium

       86.91 per cent.

The calculated percentage of cadmium

in Cd_2O_4 is:

    Cadmium

       86.79 per cent.

The determination of water in cadmium
hypoiodide was made by placing a small
specimen tube containing the hypoiodide
in a Sprengel flask which was heated
in a bath of concentrated sulphuric acid.
During the heating a slow current of dry
nitrogen was passed over the substance.

First determination of water.

Amount of substance used ---- .08434 gr.
water found ------- .₅₆.₇ ..
Water. 7.22 per cent.

Second determination of water

Amount of substance used ---- .₂8895 gr.
water found ----- ₅₆₀₀
Water. 6.7₇ per cent.

Third determination of water.

Amount of substance used ----- .1866 gr.
water found ----- .0800 .
water 7.25 per cent.

Average amount of water = 7.07 per cent.

The calculated percentage of water in
CdO_2 is, 6.99

At the temperature at which concentrated
sulphuric acid gives off dense white fumes
cadmium hydroxide gives off all its water
and passes over into a heavy yellow powder. At 150°C not a trace of water was
liberated. Under the microscope the yellow
powder was found to consist of minute
translucent crystals.

First determination of cadmium.

Amount of substance used ..... ·08?64 gr.
                cadmium found .....   ·0?5·?
    Cadmium 93.14 per cent.

Second determination of cadmium.

Amount of substance used .... ·10?46 gr.
                cadmium found .... ·10106 ?
    Cadmium 93.17 per cent.

The calculated percentage of metal in
Cd_2O is 93.32 per cent.

If water of too high temperature is
employed in washing the suboxyhydrate
the presence of free metal in it can
be detected under the microscope and

by melting between agate surfaces.
If the yellow substance is strongly heated it
breaks up into a mixture of oxide and
metal which possesses a distinctly green
color. Towards acids the suboxide conducts
itself like the silver provide.

It is a fact of some interest in connection
with the periodic arrangement of the elements, that the tendency toward the formation of a lower series of compounds, which
becomes so strongly developed in mercury,
begins to exhibit itself in some slight
degree in cadmium.

Notes on crystals of metallic Cadmium.

The measurements of the cadmium crystals were made by Dr. Williams who has very kindly furnished me with her results.

No reliable crystallographic description of the element cadmium seems thus far to have appeared – a fact due to the difficulty in obtaining suitable material. The crystals examined, although not capable of yielding entirely satisfactory results are nevertheless such as to make them of interest.

In 1852 G. Rose noted the fact that distilled cadmium collected at the neck of the retort in drops which solidified in complex polyhedral aggregates similar to those formed by zinc. In 1874 Kammerer encountered the same aggregates

which he explained as complicated iso-
metric combinations. This question
was cited in 1881 by Rammelsberg.
In 884 Brögger and Flink stated that in
their opinion zinc, magnesium and
probably cadmium were in analogy
with beryllium which they had studied,
hexagonal and isohedral. 3

This supposition has already been sub-
stantiated in the case of the two former
elements & while the present material
leads to the same result for the last
named.

The cadmium crystals were produced in
the same manner as were those of
zinc and magnesium measured before, viz; by distillation in a vacuum.
The appearance of the tubes thus stained
was very like that in the other cases.

The polyhedral aggregates were abundant and reached considerable dimensions. The crystallizing power of the cadmium however, seemed to be less, so that the only crystals suitable for measurement were extremely minute. The largest individuals were barrel-shaped, like those of zinc and resembled little piles of basal plates. Their side planes are not unfrequently uneven and bent, probably as the result of the softness and great ductility of the metal.

Only the most minute crystals show pyramidal planes of comparative perfection. These are well suited for a microscopic examination, but their small size renders their measurement on a reflecting goniometer a matter of difficulty. After a careful search two crystals were secured which, although

they had a diameter of only one third of a millimeter; from their microscopic appearances promised good results. Their planes however were found to give composed reflections and a somewhat disappointing variation in corresponding angles. On the best crystal three zones were measured as follows; (normal angles)

Zone I	Zone II	Zone III
$0001 : 0\bar{1}\bar{1} = 62°35'$	$0001 : 10\bar{1}1 = 62°4'$	$0001 : \bar{1}101 = 62°29'$
$0001 : 01\bar{1}0 = 89°00\frac{1}{2}'$		
$0001 : 01\bar{1}1 = 118°57'$	$0001 : 10\bar{1}\bar{1} = 118°28'$	

The second crystal was much less satisfactory, since values for the angle between the base and pyramid (0001) (01\bar{1}1) were obtained which varied all the way from $61°2'$ to $63°43'$. Here

measurements must therefore be regarded as of little or no value. If we average the readings for this angle on the writ crys- tal we obtain 62° 23', from which

$$\underline{a} : \underline{c} = 1 : 1.6554.$$

A comparison of the axial ratios of the four rhombohedral and four holohedral hexagonal elements gives the following:

Bismuth $\underline{a} : \underline{c} = 1 : 1.3035$ (G. Rose, 1849).

antimony $\underline{a} : \underline{c} = 1 : 1.3235$ (Laspeyres 1875).

arsenic $\underline{a} : \underline{c} = 1 : 1.3298$ (G. Rose, 1849).

mercury $\underline{a} : \underline{c} = 1 : 1.4025$ (Zepharovich 1875).

Zinc $\underline{a} : \underline{c} = 1 : 1.356425$ (Williams and Burton, 1889).

beryllium $\underline{a} : \underline{c} = 1 : 1.5812$ (Brögger, 1880).

magnesium $\underline{a} : \underline{c} = 1 : 1.6202$ (Williams, 1889).

cadmium $\underline{a} : \underline{c} = 1 : 1.6554$ (Williams, 1889).

Zinc appears from its axial ratio to be-
long rather to the rhombohedral group and
this is the only one of the last four
elements upon which the faintest indi-
cation of any divergence from a hexahedral
development in all of its forms has been
observed. In crystals of this substance
there is an occasional rhombohedral al-
ternative to the faces of certain of the
pyramids, although the crystals otherwise
appear to be hexahedral.

The crystals of cadmium like those of
magnesium show only the three forms
$OP (0001)$, $P (10\bar{1}1)$ and $\infty P (10\bar{1}0)$.
Brögger and Flink observed on beryllium
the additional forms $\infty P_2 (2\bar{1}\bar{1}0)$ and
$\tfrac{1}{2}P (20\bar{2}1)$, while upon zinc a large
number of forms in the zone of the
unit pyramid occur.

not infrequently the cadmium crystals show a tendency toward a hemimorphic development. This is plainly seen when a large number of them are examined together under the microscope. The little wedge-shaped crystals are mostly attached by their sides and yet one of their ends is often wider than the other. Sometimes they taper nearly to a point, quite like greenockite crystals.

The Cohesion Phenomena of Cadmium.

The cohesion phenomena of cadmium are similar to those of zinc but are still more striking. When a crystal is sharply viewed under the microscope and then gently pressed on the side with the point

... the ... pyramids are
be seen to suddenly become striated similar
to the ... , as though a gliding in
the basal section took place. Some of these
crystals were kindly examined by Prof.
Otto Lehmann of Karlsruhe, Germany, who
has added so much to our knowledge
of the gliding phenomena in crystals. He
has written in regard to his observations
as follows. The cadmium crystals as
far as their gliding phenomena are con-
cerned behave quite like zinc. If a crystal is carefully loosened and then squeezed
with a pair of tweezers it is easy to see
that the smooth surface where it was
attached to the glass become striated par-
allel to 0° (000) and that at the same
time two other sets of striations are produced which meet at an angle of

Biographical Sketch

_____ _____ was born near New London
Frederick County, Maryland, Nov. 1865.
After attending several schools in that
state he entered the Johns Hopkins University in the autumn of 1885 as a spe-
cial student of chemistry and physics. He
matriculated in 1887 and received the
degree of Bachelor of Arts in 1889 having
held the ordinary and an honorary
scholarship. For the last three years he has
continued his studies in the University
pursuing chemistry as a principal subject
and mineralogy and geology as subor-
dinate. During this time he has been ap-
pointed twice to a university scholarship, was
lecture assistant to Professor Remsen '90-91
and Fellow in Chemistry '91-92.